The AMAZING DAYS of ABBY HAYES

Sealed with a Kiss

ANNE MAZER

LITTLE · APPLE

SCHOLASTIC INC.
New York Toronto London Auckland
Sydney Mexico City New Delhi Hong Kong

Read more books about me!

Read more sister stories by Anne Mazer

Sister Magic

To all of Abby's fans, past, present, and future, with love

No part of this publication may be reproduced, stored in a retrieval system, or transmitted in any form or by any means, electronic, mechanical, photocopying, recording, or otherwise, without written permission of the publisher. For information regarding permission, write to Scholastic Inc., Attention: Permissions Department, 557 Broadway, New York, NY 10012.

ISBN-13: 978-0-439-82930-4
ISBN-10: 0-439-82930-5

12 11 10 9 8 7 6 5 4 3 2 1   9 10 11 12 13 14/0

Printed in the U.S.A.   40

First printing, December 2009

Chapter 1

I have discovered a truth about my older sister Eva.

It wasn't easy to understand at first. Then, when I uncovered the truth, it all made sense.

It began when Eva started talking on her cell phone constantly.

I mean, <u>every minute of the day</u>.

She was on the phone in the morning, when she came home from school, before and after dinner, and right before bedtime.

I don't attend her sports practices, but

I thought that she was probably on her phone then, too.

I bet Eva talked on her cell phone in her sleep!

Eva also became very secretive.

If she was talking on her cell and someone came into the room, Eva disappeared behind a closed door.

Or she dropped her voice to a whisper.

Sometimes she simply hung up and glared at whoever interrupted her.

And Eva was moody.

Sometimes she'd burst into song, skip down the stairs, or rush to hug me and tell me that I was the best younger sister in the world.

Then, for absolutely no reason, she'd burst into tears and shriek, "You don't get it! You'll never get it! It's hopeless!"

Mom and Dad shrugged and called it typical teenage behavior.

My little brother, Alex, didn't seem to notice anything at all.

Isabel, Eva's twin, seemed irritated, not worried. She rolled her eyes and made sarcastic remarks.

It seemed like I was the only one who was disturbed by Eva's strange new behavior.

I didn't know what to think. Was she skipping school, smoking cigarettes, or . . . what?

But that didn't make sense. Eva loves sports and everything healthy.

She's also an A student.

So why was she acting so weird?

If she had nothing to hide, why was she so secretive? And why was she ALWAYS on the phone?

Then I discovered the truth.

I'd seen it in movies and on TV, but now it was happening in my own home. It was totally obvious once I saw it.

My sister Eva was in love!

That's why she was so moody.

That's why she was on the phone all the time.

That's why she was acting so mysterious.

No one else in the family seems to have a clue. Not even Isabel.

I'm the only one who knows.

Right now, I'm keeping it secret.

Uh-oh. I have to go. It's almost time to catch the school bus.

"The drama club meeting has been moved from Tuesday after school to Thursday evening. . . ." The school secretary's voice droned from the loudspeaker. "Remember to bring in your cereal box tops next week. . . . Be sure to welcome our new assistant math teacher. . . ."

Abby stifled a yawn. Morning announcements were so boring.

Even the school secretary sounded bored as she went on about cancellations, meeting times, and lunch passes.

Abby couldn't wait until the bell rang. Even math class was preferable to this.

She glanced at Hannah in the next row. Her best friend was doodling on a piece of blank paper.

Hannah rolled her eyes. "Dullsville," she mouthed.

"I'll say," Abby muttered.

"And now, I'd like to announce a special event," the secretary said. "Valentine's Day is coming up! And so is our annual Valentine's Day dance."

Valentine's Day? A dance? The class stirred and began to come to life.

Abby had loved Valentine's Day when she was younger. She had given homemade valentines, cutout hearts, and candy to all her friends.

But now Valentine's Day was uncomfortable and awkward. She didn't know quite how she felt about it. Suddenly it was all about boys.

She had a crush on an eighth grader once. His name was Simon and he played saxophone in the Jazz Tones.

Her crush had mostly mellowed into friendship.

She didn't think about Simon all the time anymore, or long for a glimpse of him in the school hallways.

But when she ran into him, she still felt a slight glow.

It wasn't much of anything at all.

No one had ever taken Simon's place. Abby wasn't interested in any other boy. She wasn't sure that she wanted to be. She was happy the way she was. She wasn't interested in romance or anything like it.

"The dance will be held on Friday, February fourteenth," the secretary continued, "and it . . ."

The loudspeaker crackled and then died. Abby's homeroom teacher sighed.

"Not *again*," he said. "Class, you may talk quietly until the announcements come back on."

The class broke into excited whispers. Everyone wanted to talk about the dance.

Abby glanced at Hannah. She was sure that her best friend wouldn't want anything to do with a Valentine's Day dance.

Hannah wasn't that kind of girl.

"I want to go," Hannah whispered.

"With a boy?" Abby said in shock. "You, Hannah?"

"Don't be silly!" Hannah tossed her head. "I'm not talking about boys. I'm talking about going to the dance with a bunch of *friends*. Boys, girls, it doesn't matter!"

Abby let out a long breath. "But, um, isn't a Valentine's Day dance supposed to be, well, romantic?"

"It's just a middle-school dance," Hannah said. "No one is going to get too serious about it."

"I'm not sure about that," Abby said. "What about Brianna and Victoria and their friends?"

"Never mind them!" Hannah cried. "We'll dance until our shoes wear out!"

"Dances are *really* for people like Eva," Abby said. "People who are in love."

"Eva is in love?" Hannah's eyes sparkled.

Abby put her finger to her lips. "It's a secret."

"She confided in you?"

"Not really," Abby admitted.

Hannah shook her head. "Abby Hayes, I can't believe you. I'm not even going to ask how you found out."

"I wasn't snooping!" Abby protested. "I found out by accident, *really*!"

"'Accident?'" Hannah repeated.

"It wasn't my fault that Eva chose to talk near a heating vent!" Abby cried. "She practically broadcast her conversation to my room."

"Oh, yeah, sure," Hannah said.

"I was minding my own business, innocently reading a magazine in my room, when I heard her voice. . . ."

"What did you do?" Hannah asked. "Put your ear to the vent?"

Abby blushed. She hadn't *exactly* put her ear to the vent, but she had moved very close to hear what Eva was saying.

"I miss you, too," Eva had murmured. "I can hardly wait to see you again."

Abby had sat very still and listened to every word. She just couldn't help herself.

"So what if I *did* listen?" she said now. "I'm going keep Eva's secret. No one else knows. Except you."

"I won't tell," Hannah promised.

Hannah was trustworthy. And so was Abby. There was nothing to worry about.

The loudspeaker crackled again. "Sorry about the delay," the school secretary said.

The homeroom teacher rolled his eyes. "Get it fixed," he muttered.

"We have so many things to look forward to this year!" the secretary chirped. "A Valentine's Day dance . . . *and* great news! We have some very special valentines for sale.

"These adorable cards were designed by our very own eighth grade art classes," she continued. "All profits will go to buy school supplies for needy children. Buy a Smooch card and help little kids."

The boys in the class began making kissy noises.

"Quiet!" The homeroom teacher rapped on his desk. "We don't want to miss important information."

"Smooch cards will be on sale in the cafeteria and main office," the secretary said. "Buy them all. Send them to your friends. Invite your crush to the Valentine's Day dance. Say it with a Smooch card!"

Abby and Hannah exchanged another glance.

"*Say it with a Smooch card*?" Abby repeated. "What if you don't want to say *anything*?"

She especially wouldn't want to say it with a Smooch card. Not with that name.

Not even if Simon had designed every last one of them.

"I'm going to buy a ton of them," Hannah said. "If it helps little kids who don't even have pencils and crayons, I'll do it."

"Not me," Abby said stubbornly.

"Maybe you can buy some for Eva," Hannah suggested. "She can give them to her new boyfriend."

"Are you kidding?" Abby said.

"Come on, Abby! It's a silly name, but it's for a good cause."

"Well, maybe *one*," Abby said.

But only if no one was looking when she bought it.

Chapter 2

Wednesday

"Every picture tells a story."

Chalk and Blackboard Calendar

Yesterday at lunch all my classmates were gathered around the Smooch card table. It looked as if every eighth grader in the school had designed at least one. There were dozens, maybe hundreds, of Smooch cards on display.

And it was a good thing! After making fun of the name all morning, everyone suddenly decided that Smooch cards were cool.

My classmates descended on the card table in hordes.

There was such a huge crowd that I didn't feel embarrassed to be there, too.

I have to admit, I was kind of curious. Okay, I was <u>very</u> curious!

I wanted to see if Simon had designed a card.

What was it like? Did it reveal anything about him? Did his picture tell a story?

I wanted to see the other Smooch cards, too.

I wanted to see what the eighth graders had drawn and what they had written.

Most of all, I wanted to know how I would react to the Smooch cards.

How would I feel when I held one in my hands?

Would my heart start beating faster?

Would my eyes get misty?

Would I long for someone to send me a valentine? Or would I magically think of half a dozen boys to send valentines to?

I pushed my way through the crowd until I was standing in front of the card table.

The three eighth graders behind the table

were selling Smooch cards as fast as
they could.

The Smooch cards were practically flying
off the table. Everyone was snatching them up.

"Don't worry; there are plenty for
everyone," an eighth grade girl said. "We
have more in the art room."

I stared at a couple of cards on a
stand. They were typical valentine greetings
with hearts and flowers and cupids.

Other cards were scattered around the
table. They featured musical notes and
romantic quotes; birds, kittens, bumblebees,
and teddy bears; and cars, guitars,
rainbows, and stars.

There were funny messages, romantic ones,
and corny ones.

There was something for almost everyone.

But I didn't want a single one. None of
the valentines appealed to me – not even a
little.

Most of my classmates were going mad
for Smooch cards, but I was staying cool,
calm, and collected.

Was I missing out on the fun? Or

was I avoiding mass insanity? I wasn't totally sure.

One thing I WAS sure of: Either there are <u>a lot</u> of kids who want to get crayons into the hands of needy children; OR, there are a lot more kids with crushes than I ever imagined.

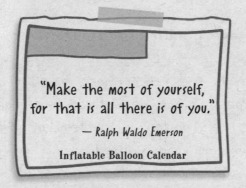

"Make the most of yourself, for that is all there is of you."

— Ralph Waldo Emerson

Inflatable Balloon Calendar

Wow. Brianna must have this advice posted on her bathroom mirror.

Brianna must always be the best, have the best, and know the best.

She ALWAYS makes the most of herself.

I bet that she writes this advice, over and over, one hundred times every morning before breakfast.

I bet she had it memorized by the time she was three years old.

I bet she has it programmed on her Me-phone.

Today Brianna was holding court near the Smooch card table.

"I've already received one hundred and fifty-two valentines," she bragged to everyone around her.

"Only one hundred and fifty-two?" Mason said.

Mason is the kid formerly known as "the Big Burper." Since he entered sixth grade, however, he's gotten a lot less obnoxious.

He saw me and winked.

"Shut up, Mason," Brianna said casually.

She pulled out her Me-phone and checked for messages. "I've just received a dozen electronic cards. The total is now one hundred and sixty-four."

Mason clutched his heart. "How can anyone compete?" he asked.

"You can't," Brianna's best friend, Victoria, said.

"I'm destroyed," Mason said.

"One hundred and sixty-seven," Brianna announced.

"Will we be getting minute by minute playbacks?" I asked under my breath. "Will there be a scoreboard in front of the school?"

"Probably," Mason said. He picked up a Smooch card and then put it down again.

"You don't seriously like Brianna, do you?" I asked.

Mason rolled his eyes. "Come on, Abby."

"Just asking," I said.

Brianna checked her appearance in a small golden mirror. "And, by the way, if anyone's thinking of asking me to the dance, I'm already taken."

"I am, too," Victoria said loudly.

In the moment of silence that followed this announcement, Mason started clapping loudly.

Brianna took a bow and resumed her bragging.

(Nothing ever stops Brianna from bragging. Not snow nor rain nor sleet nor hail.)

"Last year I got a diamond pendant," she bragged. "I got a ruby ring and a miniature chocolate yacht."

"I got a ring, too," Victoria snapped.

"Did you eat the chocolate yacht?" someone asked Brianna.

"Of course not!" Brianna said. "I'm watching my figure." She struck a model's pose for the crowd.

"Just like everyone else is," she added.

Her friends broke out in applause.

"Thank goodness there's only one Brianna, because one is already too much," I said to Mason.

But he didn't laugh at my joke like I was hoping. He had vanished into the crowd.

"There you are, Abby!" Hannah waved a Smooch card at me. "Look at what I got! Six Smooch cards! They're so cute! You have to buy some!"

I felt a bit guilty. Shouldn't I get one, at least, if only to help little kids?

"Um, I guess," I said. What would I do with a Smooch card, anyway? I'd never send a valentine to a boy. I made a list in my head:

I could play tic-tac-toe on a Smooch card.

I could use it to write down homework assignments.

I could write a very, very, very short story inside one card.

Or I could make a list of everything I disliked about Valentine's Day.

Hey! Maybe I could give one to my cat, T-Jeff.

Suddenly I had a mischievous idea.

I'd send the card as a joke.

<u>I'll give it to Eva</u>, I thought. <u>I'll pretend it's from her boyfriend and see if she's fooled.</u>

Maybe Eva would get all dreamy and happy. Maybe she'd turn on some music and dance around her room.

Maybe she'd give my Smooch card a big smooch.

I wanted to see what she'd do.

Chapter 3

What kind of a natural masterpiece is <u>my</u>
family?

Are we the awe-inspiring kind?

Would people gasp with amazement when
they first saw us?

Would they want to visit us on their
vacations?

Would they pay seventeen dollars to camp
out in our dining room and watch us eat
dinner and argue every night?

Would the government declare that we
are a "protected environment"?

<u>I</u> need a protected environment!!

I'm in trouble and it's all because I played an innocent joke!

(Shouldn't pranks and jokes be part of our natural family masterpiece? My sister Eva doesn't think so. . . .)

Last night I wrote a romantic message inside the Smooch card, signed it with lots of love and kisses from "you know who," and slipped it under Eva's door.

I felt very clever for about fifteen minutes. Then Eva stormed into my room.

"Okay, what's the big idea, Abby?"

I tried to act innocent. "Huh?"

"I can recognize your handwriting from a mile away! Even if you try to disguise it," my older sister said.

"A mile away? Really?" I said.

"Don't change the subject!" Eva snapped.

"What is the subject?"

My sister threw the Smooch card at me. It landed in my lap. "This is!"

I picked up the card and pretended to examine it. "You must really love me. You're throwing valentines at me."

"Shut up. That's not funny."

"I think it is." I dropped the card on the floor between us.

Eva folded her arms across her chest. "You sent me this card, Abby. It's a cruel, sick joke."

"It's a harmless, innocent prank," I said. "So what if I sent it to you?"

"It's . . . it's . . . mean and rotten!"

"Mean and rotten? What are you talking about?"

Had love made Eva completely lose her sense of humor?

"Can't you take a joke?" I said.

Eva glared at me.

"It's just a card." I said. "It's not like I wore your favorite sweater or lost your lacrosse stick or made you miss your practice."

"You don't know . . ." Eva said.

Oh, yes, I do, I wanted to say. But I figured she'd get really mad.

"And if you ever do anything like this again . . ."

Eva didn't bother to finish her sentence. She slammed the door behind her as she left.

"It backfired!" were Abby's first words to Hannah when her best friend picked up her cell phone.

"Oh, no!" Hannah wailed. And then, "What backfired?"

Abby let out a long sigh. It was good to hear Hannah's voice on the other end of the line.

Thank goodness for cell phones! She could call Hannah whenever she wanted.

And she never had to wait for a free line, or worry about someone listening in on another phone.

Like Eva. Or Isabel. Or Alex.

"Remember the Smooch card I bought?" Abby asked her.

"I do," Hannah said.

"Well, I sent it to Eva as a joke. I pretended it was from her boyfriend."

"Why did you do *that*?"

"I didn't know who else to send it to."

"What about *me*?"

"I should have thought of that."

Didn't her mother always say, "Hindsight is twenty-twenty"? That meant you always knew what to do *after* you had made the mistake.

It was easy to see things when it was too late.

"Now Eva's really mad. She threw the Smooch card at me," Abby confessed.

"Wow," Hannah said. "That's amazing."

"Amazing?" Abby repeated. "That's not the word I'd use."

Was it aggravating? Awful? Appalling?

Hannah didn't know what it felt like to fight and argue all the time. She didn't have older siblings, just a baby sister who was ten years younger.

Hannah was more like her aunt than a big sister. She took care of her little sister; she didn't throw Smooch cards at her.

Sometimes Abby wished that she wasn't a middle child in a family of squabbling, noisy siblings.

Life would be so much easier if she had an adorable baby sister like Elena.

"How did your fight end?" Hannah asked.

"I told Eva that she had lost her sense of humor. She stormed out," Abby said with a shrug.

"Why did she have to get so angry?" she added. "It was just a stupid joke!"

As far as Abby was concerned, *Valentine's Day* was a stupid joke. She didn't get it.

"Maybe Eva was upset about something else," Hannah suggested.

"But what?"

"*I* think . . ." Hannah began, but she was interrupted by a pulsing sound. "I have another call coming in," she said.

"Call me back," Abby said, and pressed the END button.

That was what she *didn't* like about cell phones. Someone was always interrupting. Or texting. Land lines had call waiting, too, but somehow they never seemed as busy.

Abby looked around her room. The Smooch card she sent Eva was still lying on the floor.

She picked it up and threw it in the wastebasket. "What a fuss over nothing," she muttered.

There was a light tap on the door. Isabel poked her head in the room. "Can I come in?" she asked.

"Um, yes," Abby said. She took a deep breath and tried to remember if she had done anything to annoy the other twin lately.

She hoped that Isabel wasn't going to complain.

Abby hadn't borrowed her nail polish lately, or worn her clothes, or taken one of her books.

But if she *had* done something, Isabel would let her know. She never minced words.

Isabel always had plenty to say — and she never hesitated to say it.

But Isabel didn't say a word. She sat down cross-legged on Abby's bed and stared at the wall.

Was she in love, too, Abby wondered?

That would be seriously weird. Abby didn't know if she could stand it.

"What's up?" she said.

"Eva," Isabel replied.

Abby was startled. That wasn't what she expected to hear. Had Eva told Isabel about the Smooch card? Had she sent Isabel to scold Abby?

"It was just a prank," Abby began.

Isabel cut her off. "I don't know what you're talking about," she said with a wave of her hand. "But I have more serious concerns."

"Serious?" Abby repeated.

"Eva's been acting funny."

"Um, yeah," Abby said. She knew the reason why, but she didn't know whether she should tell Isabel.

"Eva's a teen, isn't she?" Abby said.

Isabel gave her a look. "What would *you* know about *that*?"

"Plenty!" Abby retorted. "I have to live with two of you."

Isabel ignored the insult. She brooded some more.

"I'm worried," Isabel finally said.

Abby looked at her in amazement. "I thought . . ." Her voice trailed off.

She hadn't thought Isabel had noticed. But she should have known better.

"I think you're worried, too," Isabel added.

I am! Abby wanted to cry. Or, *I used to be — until I discovered Eva's secret.*

Maybe she really ought to tell Isabel. It would ease her mind. But she held back.

Was it right to reveal someone else's secret?

"I'm her twin," Isabel said. "I know something is wrong. Do you have any idea what it is?"

Yes, Abby wanted to say. *She's in love.*

She wanted to tell Isabel about the phone call she had overheard, the card she had sent, and how furious Eva had been.

If I tell her, maybe she'd help me understand, she thought.

But she couldn't tell. It wasn't like Eva was in danger. Or as if something was *seriously* wrong.

It was a private thing.

Besides, it was never a good idea to tell one twin the other's secrets.

"You know something," Isabel said suddenly. "I can feel it in my bones."

"Then get an X-ray, ha, ha, ha."

"You're not funny, Abby."

Abby sighed. "Doesn't anyone around here appreciate my sense of humor?"

"Come on!" Isabel urged. "Why don't you tell me what's going on."

Abby took a deep breath. "I can't," she said.

"At least tell me if she's okay!"

"Um, I think so," Abby said. Then she had an inspiration. "Why don't you ask her yourself?"

Isabel stood up. "Why do you think I came here?"

"To annoy me?"

"Eva won't say a word!" Isabel cried. "She won't tell me anything!"

Abby looked at her. "I'm sorry," she said.

"If you feel like talking, I'll be in my room." Isabel hurried out of the room. Unlike Eva, she didn't slam the door behind her.

Chapter 4

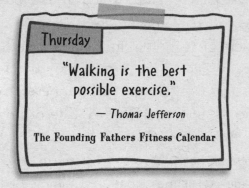

Thursday

"Walking is the best possible exercise."

— *Thomas Jefferson*

The Founding Fathers Fitness Calendar

Then why are we running? Will someone please give this quote to the gym teacher?

She won't listen to me, but I think she'd listen to Thomas Jefferson.

He can tell her what a stupid idea it is to spend our gym classes running around  and around and around and around and around. . . .

Okay, I know it's February and we can't go outside, but isn't there something better to do?

Like yoga or square dancing or jousting?

Can we please stop doing these pathetic imitations of a hamster in a cage?

I'm sick of running in circles! And we're not even all going in the same direction!

There are five groups of runners, and each one is sprinting in an alternating direction from the next.

It makes me feel as if I'm in the middle of a huge whirling daisy. I immediately got so dizzy that I had to sit down.

And then I pulled out my journal to write a few words.

That was a good idea!

But I don't think the gym teacher agrees. She's headed over here with a dangerous look in her eye.

Uh-oh. I might have to stop wri..........

"Why are you sitting down, Hayes? Are you sick?" the gym teacher demanded. "Do you need to go to the nurse's office?"

"I'm just taking a rest," Abby said, slipping her journal quickly into her backpack.

"If there's nothing wrong with you, get up and run," the teacher ordered her. "I don't allow any slacking in my class."

What's wrong with a little slacking? Abby thought.

Her English teacher wouldn't call her a slacker. She'd call her "highly motivated" instead.

It was all a matter of perspective.

Would the gym teacher agree? Probably not.

Abby got to her feet. She wasn't going to argue.

She was lucky that the teacher hadn't made a bigger deal of her writing during gym class.

"Sorry," she mumbled. With a sigh, she jogged back onto the track and joined the stream of running bodies.

"Are you okay?" Hannah asked as she passed in the other direction.

"Yeah," Abby said. There wasn't time to say anything more. She lined herself up behind a slow-moving jogger and tried to match his pace.

If she were careful, maybe she wouldn't get dizzy again.

"Round one," she said to herself as she ran. She glanced at the clock. "Only twenty-nine minutes left."

She wished there was music. Loud, pulsing music would make this so much easier.

But there was no sound other than the pounding of sneakered feet and hard breathing.

Mason came hurling around the track from the other direction. When he saw her, his eyes lit up.

"Didn't get away with it, did you?" he teased. "I saw you writing in that journal!"

Abby just had time to make a face at him. And then he was gone.

Sophia ran past her next. Her face was flushed and sweaty. She held up two fingers in a peace sign as she passed.

Abby concentrated on the back of the person in front of her and paced herself.

If she could get into a rhythm, this wouldn't be so bad.

Brianna zoomed past. "I could do this in my sleep," she bragged.

"I'd rather sleep," Abby retorted.

Mason came around again.

"You're *way* too fast!" Abby said. "You're setting a bad example for the rest of us!"

"What's the matter? Don't you like jogging?"

"I prefer walking," she said.

Mason waved as he sprinted past. Had he even heard her answer?

Abby glanced at the clock. Twenty-seven minutes to go. Time was passing too slowly.

"I'm getting winded!" Sophia huffed as they passed again.

"I was winded before I even started!" Abby said.

"Faster!" the gym teacher called, clapping her hands.

Sweat was starting to pour into Abby's eyes. She wiped it away and picked up her pace. Everyone seemed to be running faster than her.

Even the slow boy in front of her had disappeared.

"I love this," Hannah said as she sailed around a corner.

Abby just shook her head. She glanced at the clock again. Only a minute had gone by.

"I have new trainers," Brianna bragged as she passed Abby again. She pointed to her sneakers. They were glittery gold.

"You mean new sneakers!" Abby said. "Those are plain, ordinary, golden *sneakers*, Brianna."

"You tell her," Mason said. His laugh rose above the pounding of the runners.

"Keep moving!" the gym teacher called. "You, Hayes, less talking, more running!"

Abby began to run for real. She didn't want to get into any more trouble with the gym teacher today.

"You're too quiet, Hayes," Mason said, nudging her with his arm the next time they passed each other.

"Don't get me in trouble!" Abby warned. But she smiled at Mason as she said it.

"Pick up that pace!" he teased. He jogged in place for a moment. "See if you can beat me."

Abby shook her head. Mason ran on the track team. "No way!" she cried. "Besides, we're running in opposite directions."

"Picky, picky." Mason took off again.

Abby put on a burst of speed.

"Way to go, Abby!" Hannah said as she flew by.

"I'd like to just *go*," Abby groaned.

"To a spa or a tropical island," Sophia finished. Her dark ponytail bounced on her back.

"Yes!" Abby agreed. "Anywhere but here."

"Awww . . . I thought you liked it here," Mason said. He was passing her again.

"You again?" Abby said. "I see you more than anyone else."

"That's because I'm faster than anyone else."

He was gone as soon as he spoke.

It was true. Mason was faster. And he was funnier, too, for that matter.

"Starting to enjoy this?" Hannah asked, sprinting past.

"Maybe," Abby said.

She realized with surprise that she *was* starting to enjoy the class.

Running was more comfortable now. She didn't have to think about it or push herself. She had found her rhythm.

"Good work, Hayes," the gym teacher said. "Keep it up."

Abby put on another brief burst of speed.

It was also good to trade jokes with Mason, to complain to Sophia, and to see Hannah's smile.

And *no one* had spoken about Valentine's Day dances or Smooch cards once during the entire class.

For the first time in her life, Abby wished that gym class would last forever. Couldn't she stay here for the next few weeks?

At least until Valentine's Day was over?

Chapter 5

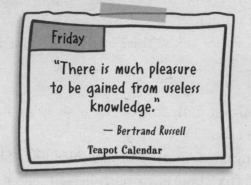

Friday

"There is much pleasure to be gained from useless knowledge."

— Bertrand Russell

Teapot Calendar

WRONG!!!

There is _NO_ pleasure to be gained from useless knowledge.

Useless knowledge: Eva is in love.

So where is the pleasure?

One: I haven't been able to tease Eva.

Two: I haven't gotten Eva to do my chores.

Three: I haven't dropped any tantalizing hints to Isabel.

There's been <u>no</u> pleasure gained at all.

In fact, it's the opposite.

Isabel thinks I'm holding out on her. Eva is mad at me.

This knowledge isn't useless!

It's worse than useless! It's uncomfortable, awkward, and it gets me in trouble with my siblings.

It was the middle of the school day. Abby hurried from one class to another, trying to avoid looking at the Smooch cards.

They now reminded her not only of Valentine's Day, but also of her older sisters. And *that* reminded her that they were both very annoyed with her.

Somehow she had gotten put in the middle again. Was that because she was a middle child?

Abby sighed as another Smooch card reared up in front of her. This one was dangling from a seventh grade girl's backpack.

Smooch cards were everywhere.

Original Smooch card artwork was on display in the cafeteria; teachers had thumbtacked Smooch cards to their bulletin boards.

Students glued them on notebook covers and were hanging them in their lockers, and one boy had even made a hat out of Smooch cards.

Everyone in middle school seemed to be buying them, displaying them, or exchanging them.

"What's the matter, Abby?" Sophia asked. "You look upset about something."

Sophia's long, dark hair was pulled into a ponytail. Her backpack was decorated with slogans and buttons.

Sophia wanted to be an artist. She spent every spare moment drawing in a blank notebook she carried everywhere.

"Oh, it's nothing," Abby said. "Just an overdose of Smooch cards, that's all."

"But they're so cute!" Sophia cried. "And so romantic, too!"

"And they help buy school supplies for little kids," Abby finished with a sigh. "I know all about it."

Brianna interrupted them.

"Hey, everyone," she began. "I have an important announcement!"

"Oh, really?" Abby said.

Brianna only made important announcements about one subject: herself.

"I have a new outfit for the Valentine's Day dance," she bragged. "A gold cashmere sweater, a matching flounced skirt — and even a new coat."

"Congratulations," Sophia said.

Brianna flashed her broadest movie star smile. Then she waltzed over to another group of girls to tell them the news.

"Brought to you by the Brianna Channel," Abby said in a fake newscaster voice. "All Brianna, all the time."

"If it doesn't exist, Brianna will soon start it," Sophia commented.

"What were we talking about?" Abby said. "Before Brianna interrupted us, I mean."

"I forgot."

"Smooch cards," Abby said. She made a face. She shouldn't have brought up the subject again. Oh, well. "Have you gotten any?"

"Not yet," Sophia said. "But I've sent a few."

"To *boys*?" Abby said in astonishment.

She couldn't believe it. Sophia was very shy. "Or *a* boy?"

Sophia suddenly looked embarrassed. "Well, uh, yeah . . ."

"Who?" Abby asked.

Sophia shook her head.

"I get it," Abby said. "You want to keep it secret. My sister . . ."

She stopped herself. She couldn't blurt out Eva's secret to anyone else.

"Are you going to the dance?" Abby said to change the subject. "Hannah is getting a group of friends together."

Sophia's blush deepened.

"You're going with a *boy*?"

"I don't know," Sophia admitted. "I hope so."

"Wow," Abby said. "Wow." She didn't know what else to say.

"Are you going?" Sophia asked her.

"I don't think so," Abby choked out.

"Not even with Hannah?" Sophia said.

Abby shook her head.

"Are you going to hide out until February fifteenth?" Sophia asked. "Or wear a paper bag over your head?"

"Why can't things stay the same?" Abby burst out. "I liked Valentine's Day the way it *used* to be."

Sophia was quiet for a moment. "I like all the changes," she admitted. "I like this part of growing up."

The bell rang.

"Are you going to study hall?" Sophia asked.

"I'm going to my locker to get some books first," Abby said.

The two girls waved to each other and hurried off in opposite directions.

Abby fiddled with the catch on the lock. Why did it *always* stick when she was in a hurry?

She missed elementary school, where nobody had lockers.

After the third try, it released. Abby yanked the door open, grabbed the books she needed, and was about to slam the door shut again.

But then she saw the envelope.

She leaned over to pick it up. She didn't recognize the handwriting.

It looked like an invitation to a party — hopefully not a Valentine's Day party.

Abby turned it over. There was no return address or name on the envelope.

Then she tore it open. And stared in shock.

Someone had sent her a Smooch card.

It was one of the more romantic cards, covered with flowers and birds and hearts.

She opened the card.

HAPPY VALENTINE'S DAY, the card read. WILL YOU BE MY VALENTINE?

Abby's heart pounded. Was this some kind of joke? Or was this for real?

For a moment, she couldn't breathe. Then, slowly, she let out a long breath.

It was signed SEALED WITH A KISS, FROM YOUR SECRET ADMIRER.

Chapter 6

> **Friday, study hall**
>
> "Anyone who isn't confused really doesn't understand the situation."
>
> — Edward R. Murrow
>
> **Network Calendar**

I am confused.

So, does that mean I actually understand the situation?

But I don't understand the situation AND I'm confused!

Does it mean I actually _do_ understand it?

Or am I just plain confused?

This quote makes me feel more confused than ever! And I don't understand the situation at all.

*   *   *

I'm supposed to be studying for a social studies quiz, but I can't stop thinking about the Smooch card I just found in my locker.

I'll take a Smooch card quiz instead.

<u>Smooch card quiz:</u>

1. Did someone actually send me, Abby Hayes, a Smooch card?

Answer: Yes. It is in my backpack. I look at it every five minutes to make sure that I didn't imagine it.

2. Does a boy have a crush on me?

Answer: Yes. He wrote, "Will you be my valentine?" What else is that but a crush?

3. Do I really have a secret admirer?

Answer: Well, duh. Why else did he sign the Smooch card "your secret admirer"?

4. Who is he?

Answer: Could be any boy in middle school. That means there are hundreds of possibilities.

5. Could it be Simon?

Answer: As my science teacher says, "theoretically, yes."

*   *   *

Fact: I HAVE A SECRET ADMIRER.
Fact: HE SENT ME A SMOOCH CARD.
Fact: HE WROTE, "WILL YOU BE MY VALENTINE?"
Fact: HE SEALED IT WITH A KISS!

Do I dare hope?
Could it be him?
Could Simon possibly have a crush on me?

We pause for a daydream. Walking down the hall with Simon, he compliments me on my curly red hair.

No, wait! Who in his right mind would compliment this wild mess of red curls?

Start again.

Walking down the hall with Simon, he compliments me on my lovely musical laugh.

(Note to self: Practice laugh at home. No snorting or guffawing. Try to make it more bell-like and tinkling.)

He gazes adoringly into my eyes and says . . .

*   *   *

Stop! What are you thinking, Abby Hayes?

Of course it isn't Simon!

He never stops or even pauses when he sees me in the hallway! All he does is smile and wave.

He doesn't go out of his way to talk to me.

He doesn't make a beeline for me in a crowd.

His eyes don't light up when he sees me.

Is that the way an eighth grader with a crush behaves?

I don't think so.

Besides, he wouldn't have a crush on _me_. He'd fall for another musician, someone who plays in the Jazz Tones, or in the school orchestra.

And his crush would be in seventh or eighth grade. NOT in sixth grade like me!

P.S. I don't really have a crush on him anymore, anyway. So why am I getting so dreamy about Simon?

More Questions:

1.   If Simon doesn't have a crush on me, who does?

Answer: I don't know.

2. Is it someone I know?

Answer: I don't know.

3. Is it someone who's seen me in the hallways?

Answer: I don't know.

4. What do I do about it?

Answer: I don't know.

Yes, I'm confused. No, I don't understand anything about this situation.

Note to self: Forget it. It's just a Smooch card.

Another note to self: "Just" a Smooch card? It's the first romantic card I've ever gotten in my life! How can I forget it?

A third note to self: Ask friends, Hannah and Sophia, for help and advice.

A fourth note to self: What if they laugh? What if they think it's silly?

Fifth note to self: Forget it. Didn't I already tell you that?

Sixth note to self: Shut up.

Seventh note to self: Stop writing notes to self. Now!!

Friday, one hour later

Found another Smooch card in my locker. My first thought: Someone is mixing up my locker number with Brianna's or Victoria's.

But my name is written on the envelope. The Smooch card is for me.

Opened it.

This one has kittens on the front. Secret admirer drew arrow pointing to one of the kittens and wrote T-JEFF.

Smooch card definitely not intended for Brianna.

Secret admirer knows me.

Secret admirer knows my cat.

* * *

Friday, two hours later

A third Smooch card! Is this a joke, or something?

This one has a big heart on it. Inside it reads YOU HAVE THE CUTEST SMILE IN THE SCHOOL. BE MY VALENTINE. S.W.A.K.

I don't think it's a joke.

Friday, half an hour later

Rush to locker to see if there's another Smooch card. There isn't.

Feel strangely disappointed.

Friday, end of school day

Have checked locker too many times today. Starting to get odd looks from other students.

Must find excuse for excessive locker looking and locking.

Like, I have to exercise the door hinges.

Or, I have a rare illness only cured by slamming locker doors.

Or, my locker is lonely. It misses me when I'm in class.

Oh, never mind!

Friday, absolutely last time I'll check before I get on the school bus

Hooray! Hooray! Hooray!

There's another Smooch card in my locker.

This one has musical notes. It reads YOU MAKE MY HEART SING.

(Could it be someone in the band? A friend of Simon's?)

<u>My</u> heart is singing!

Wait a minute!

Stop, right now!

I don't like Smooch cards. I don't like Valentine's Day and all that romantic stuff.

Remember?

So how come I'm ripping open Smooch cards and checking my locker every five minutes?

Has my secret admirer changed my personality in one day?

*   *   *

Friday, late afternoon, in my room

Suddenly I had a horrid thought.
Maybe Eva did this?
Maybe she sent me Smooch cards today to pay me back for the trick I played on her?
Could she have? Would she have?
Okay, the handwriting is different, but she could have disguised it, or had one of her guy friends write the messages. She knows some eighth grade guys from the swim team.
I went to her room and banged on the door.
When she opened it, I held up one of the Smooch cards. (Not the one that read YOU HAVE THE CUTEST SMILE IN THE SCHOOL.)
"Is this from you?" I demanded.
"No," Eva said. She tried to slam the door, but I pushed my way into her room.
"Disappear, Abby."
"Not until you answer my question," I said. "Did you send me any Smooch cards today?"
"Why would I do that?" she said. "I'm not immature, Abby. I would never send

an anonymous card to my sister and pretend it was from a guy."

"I'm sorry, already," I said.

"You should be."

"You really didn't do it?" I said again.

"Get lost, Abby." Eva looked longingly at
her cell phone. She probably wanted to call
her boyfriend.

"I'm not as immature as you think," I
said. I wanted to tell Eva that I had
protected her secret.

Except that she doesn't know that I
KNOW her secret. That was a whole other
conversation that I wasn't ready to have
right now.

I went back to my room. I was kind of
relieved that Eva hadn't sent the Smooch
cards.

That meant that I DID have a secret
admirer.

Even if I wasn't absolutely sure I
wanted one.

Chapter 7

Do they?

I have received four Smooch cards from my secret admirer. Well, it's five now.

I found another one in my locker this morning.

I feel all mixed up. Am I happy about this? Am I nervous? Am I pleased or displeased? Who's sending the cards, anyway?

I _had_ to talk to my friends! I was sure they'd understand. I thought they'd help me sort out my feelings.

But we didn't seem to have much in common.

Hannah:
"But I thought you weren't into valentines," she kept saying. "I thought you hated that sort of thing."

"I do, but I don't," I tried to explain. "I mean, I really sort of dislike valentines, but I also kind of like it that someone has a crush on me, even if I don't think I really want them to."

"That doesn't make any sense," Hannah said. "If you don't like the Smooch cards, ignore them. If you do, then enjoy them. . . ."

"It's not that simple," I said.

"But it is," Hannah insisted.

Sophia:
"You have a secret admirer?" she said enviously. "You are so lucky!"

"But I don't know who it is," I said.

"You probably do."

"I don't even know whether I want a secret admirer. . . ."

"How could anyone be unhappy about a secret admirer?" Sophia insisted.

Brianna:
No, I didn't tell her. Do you think I'm nuts? Besides, I know what she'd say:
"He must have mixed up the lockers. That card was meant for ME. So hand it over, Abby!"

Victoria:
I didn't tell the meanest girl in sixth grade, either.
She'd probably just sneer.
And then she'd tell everyone.
If I told Victoria, the entire school would tease me about my secret admirer.
I'd have to go hide in a cave until after Valentine's Day.

Mason:
Yes, I actually asked a boy.
He just kind of grinned at me.
"Stop laughing!" I ordered him. "That's no help!"

"Okay, I'll be serious," Mason promised. He stroked his chin and pretended to think. "Do you like your secret admirer?"

"How should I know? It's a secret admirer. _Secret_, Mason," I said again for emphasis. "That means I have no clue who it is!"

"Positive?" Mason said.

"Yes."

"You really don't?"

"Why does no one listen to me?" I cried.

I wish my friends had more in common with me.

I wish they understood what it's like to have a secret admirer – especially a secret admirer that I didn't expect and am not sure that I want.

I mean, I _think_ I don't want one. I don't know!

But when I pass boys in the hallway, I can't help looking at them differently.

I look at every single boy and wonder: Are _you_ my secret admirer?

Chapter 8

"Everything you can
imagine is real."

— Pablo Picasso

Blue Calendar

Everything?
If this is true, I'm in trouble.

Everything I can imagine (a short list):

1. That my secret admirer is six or seven different boys

2. That my secret admirer is a close friend

3. That my secret admirer is someone I'd never think of

4. That my secret admirer will/won't stop sending me Smooch cards

5. That my secret admirer will/won't ask me to the Valentine's Day dance

6. That I'll never figure out who my secret admirer is
7. That my secret admirer is a hoax
8. That all my friends think I'm crazy
9. That I AM crazy

Is ALL this real? I truly hope not!!!

The final bell was ringing as Abby hurried into art class. She smiled at the teacher.

Ms. Bean was her favorite middle-school teacher. She didn't look much older than her students. Today, she was wearing paint-splattered khaki pants and a green T-shirt. Her hair was pinned messily on top of her head with colorful clips.

Abby slid into her seat and put down her backpack.

"I know that everyone is excited about Valentine's Day," Ms. Bean began, "so just for fun, we're going to make our own valentines today."

Cheers broke out in the class. Only Abby covered her face with her hands. Would she never get away from this holiday?

"No!" she groaned.

"We're going to do something a little different,

though," Ms. Bean went on. "We're going to make valentines for someone we'd never send one to."

"My little brother?" someone said.

"The mailman?"

"The cafeteria ladies!"

"Our president!"

"All of those are good suggestions," Ms. Bean said. "You could even send one to your worst enemy."

She began passing out supplies: red, pink, and white paper, along with lace doilies, glitter pens, glue, markers, paints, and scissors.

"Here you are, Abby," Ms. Bean said, handing her some paper, doilies, and scissors.

"This is *so* elementary school," Abby muttered.

But no one else in the class seemed to mind. At least Abby didn't have to make a valentine for a crush . . . or her secret admirer!

Next to her, Hannah was already starting to color a valentine for the librarian. It featured lots of books arranged in a heart shape.

And Mason was cutting out a folding card for his uncle.

Brianna began to design a gigantic valentine for herself. "Everyone always sends *me* Valentines," she said. "Why not make one for myself for a change?"

"Her whole life is one long valentine to herself," Abby murmured.

Mason snickered. "Who are *you* making one for?" he asked. "Me?"

"You wish!" Abby teased. "I'm sending an anti-valentine to Valentine's Day."

"*What?*"

"Never mind," Abby said. The words had just popped out of her mouth. She didn't know what they meant, either. "You'll see."

She grabbed a sheet of pink paper and cut out a large heart. Then she cut it up with a pair of scissors. She glued the ripped pieces of the heart to another pink heart, added some bits of lace, scribbled around the edges with a pink glitter pen, and then wrote TO VALENTINE'S DAY on it.

Underneath, in regular pen, she wrote:

Ten Reasons Why I Don't Like You:

1. You are gooey and mushy.
2. Everyone forgets themselves whenever you show up.
3. Secret admirers are on the loose!
4. Why are you such a big deal?

5. If you had any sense, you'd keep the chocolate and skip the dances, cards, and sweet talk.

6. We should have left you in elementary school, where you were fun.

7. You don't go away when I tell you to.

8. I hate pink! (I hope you noticed that this valentine is TOTALLY pink.)

9. My friends all love you.

10. I don't know what to do — about you or my secret admirer!

Ms. Bean laughed out loud when she saw Abby's valentine. "This is the most original one yet," she said.

Abby blushed. "Really?"

"I'd like to hang it up for everyone to see," Ms. Bean said. "Okay?"

Abby shook her head. She didn't want everyone to know how she felt about her secret admirer.

She didn't want everyone to know she *had* a secret admirer! They might tease her, or worse.

Ms. Bean smiled. "That's fine if you want to keep it to yourself. I understand." She passed on to the next student.

Hannah leaned over to read Abby's valentine. "It's really funny," she said.

"This secret admirer business is driving me crazy," Abby said. "It's not funny at all."

"You *really* don't have a clue who it is?" Mason asked.

"He's a mystery man," Abby said. "Or a mystery boy . . ."

"We'll help you figure out who he is," Sophia offered. She was holding a beautiful valentine that she had drawn for a neighbor. "Right, Hannah?"

Hannah nodded. "Of course we will."

"That would be awesome," Abby said.

"Tell us everything you know about the secret admirer," Hannah said. "Give us all the clues you can."

"He likes to send Smooch cards," Abby said, tightening the cap on a glue stick. "He knows where my locker is. And, oh, yeah, he knows T-Jeff."

Sophia grabbed a sheet of paper and a Magic Marker. "Let's make a list of likely candidates," she said.

"Candidates?" Abby said. "Sounds like he's running for president."

"President of your heart," Mason teased.

"My secret admirer might write that," Abby said.

Hannah and Sophia looked at each other.

"Mason? Are *you* Abby's secret admirer?" they asked.

Mason grinned widely. "Yes, it's me."

"Oh, sure," Abby said. She put her glue stick inside the desk and banged the lid shut. "Cross *him* off the list."

"You'll be sorry," Mason said.

"I don't think so!" Abby retorted. She gave Mason a friendly push.

"What about Simon?" Sophia asked.

Abby shook her head.

"Simon? That silly saxophone player?" Mason frowned.

"He's not silly!" Abby protested. "He's a very serious person."

"A seriously silly saxophonist?" Mason said.

"Shush, Mason," Hannah said. "We have work to do here. Abby, what about Zach or Tyler?"

"Only if one of them mistook me for the latest online game," Abby said.

Mason snickered.

Sophia's eyes lit up. "I know who it is! That editor on *The Daisy*."

"You mean Lucas?" Abby said in dismay. "You're kidding, right?"

Lucas was sarcastic, messy, and wrote poems about old linoleum floors.

"I really think he likes you," Sophia said.

"I hope not," Abby said, "but he'd never send a Smooch card, anyway. He'd send me a picture of a dead mouse, or something."

"Ugh," Sophia said.

"Exactly," Abby agreed.

"What's wrong with dead mice?" Mason asked.

"Don't you have *anything* helpful to say?" Hannah said to Mason.

Mason folded his arms across his chest. "I have only one name for you: Casey."

Abby took a deep breath.

Casey was one of her oldest friends. But she hadn't seen him much lately. He was on another team and their schedules didn't mesh.

"Casey," she said slowly. "I wonder . . ."

"No, it's not him." Hannah sounded quite definite. "Never. He would have said something to me."

"Oh, really?" Mason said.

This time it was Hannah's turn to blush.

Abby stared at her friend for a moment. Could Hannah have a crush?

"Never mind," Hannah mumbled.

"I don't think that it's Casey," Sophia said. "I mean, he's a friend. Wouldn't he just come out and say it?"

"Maybe," Mason said. "Maybe not."

Abby threw her hands up. "We're no closer to my secret admirer's real identity."

"We could have the envelopes fingerprinted," Hannah suggested.

"By whom?" Abby demanded. "One of Brianna's cousin's nephew's wife's uncle's grandmother's best friend's detective's daughters?"

"Ha-ha," said Mason.

"Why don't you go up to random guys and ask them?" Sophia said.

"*Never!*" Abby cried in horror.

"Put Brianna herself on the case," Hannah slyly suggested. "She'll alert the entire school."

"And steal my secret admirer for herself," Abby said.

"Is it that cute guy in study hall?" Sophia said with a sigh. "You know, the one with the ponytail?"

"Not him!" Abby cried. "He doesn't know T-Jeff."

"Maybe someone told him about T-Jeff?" Hannah suggested.

"That's a stretch," Abby said. The mystery was driving her crazy.

The bell rang. The four friends gathered up their backpacks and headed out into the hallway.

We'll never figure this out, Abby thought. *Not unless the secret admirer hands me a Smooch card in person.*

Chapter 9

Thursday

"Every picture tells
a story."

Chalk and Blackboard Calendar

I know, I know. I just used this quote
in my journal a few days ago. But I just
HAVE to use it again.

Something strange has happened.
It's as if my secret admirer has read
my mind.
Or maybe someone told him that I'm
dying to know his identity?
My secret admirer has started leaving
clues in the Smooch cards.
"Clues?" you say. "How do you know
they're clues?"

Well, actually, I don't. But what else can they be?

Here's what I've found in my last three Smooch cards:

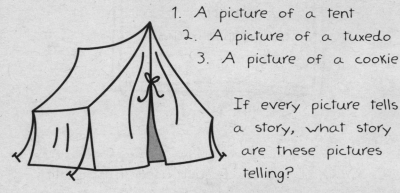

1. A picture of a tent
2. A picture of a tuxedo
3. A picture of a cookie

If every picture tells a story, what story are these pictures telling?

Guesses:
Clue: tent. Guess: He's a Boy Scout.
Clue: tux. Guess: He likes formal dances and good manners.
Clue: cookie. Guess: He has a sweet tooth. He thinks <u>I'm</u> sweet?

More Guesses:
He has a tent in his backyard?
He has good intentions?

*   *   *

Never mind!

When I told Sophia what I was
thinking, she laughed so hard that tears
came into her eyes.

"You're on the wrong track," she finally
said.

"How do you know?"

"Sixth sense," she said. "Or maybe
common sense."

"I just don't understand why he doesn't
tell me who he is."

Mason joined the two of us. "Maybe he's
shy," he suggested.

"Then he's definitely not you," I said.

Mason smiled in a knowing way.

"What?" I said.

"What what?" Mason said.

"You know my secret admirer," I said.
The words flew out of my mouth. I didn't
even know why I had said them.

But Mason didn't deny it. "So what if
I do?"

I stared at him in surprise. "You really know something, don't you?" I said. I wondered again if it was Casey.

"Did you tell him to start leaving clues for me?" I asked.

Mason shrugged.

"Tell me who it is," I pleaded. "Please, Mason, please, please."

"That's for me to know and you to find out."

No matter how hard I begged, he wouldn't say another word.

After this conversation with Mason, I took another look at the pictures my secret admirer had sent me.

But they refused to tell their story.

Mason isn't talking — and neither are they!

I'm not any closer to finding out the identity of my secret admirer.

But Mason knows.

He knows something.

Has he known all along and not told me?

Or did he find out by accident?

Maybe he caught my secret admirer in the act of slipping a Smooch card into my locker.

Or maybe it's one of his close friends, or even an acquaintance.

Must keep an eye on Mason.

Must watch who he talks to. Must note whom he eats lunch with.

It won't be hard to do.

He's always hanging out with US lately!

After dinner, Abby went up to Isabel's room.

"What is it?" Isabel asked, coming to the door with a book in her hand. "I have a test to study for."

Abby thrust three pictures into her hand. "This won't take long," she said. "Just tell me what these pictures remind you of."

"A tent, a tux, and a cookie?" Isabel said. "Is this some kind of guessing game?"

"Sort of," Abby said. "I need to know if they make you think of one of my guy friends."

Isabel gave her a look.

"Oh, and here's a diving board, too," Abby added before her sister could say anything.

It was the latest one. She had found it in another Smooch card at the end of the school day.

"And you're asking me this because . . . ?" Isabel asked.

"Um, long story," Abby said.

"Whatever," Isabel said. She arranged the pictures on her desk and studied them.

Abby crossed her fingers.

She hoped that Isabel would help.

Abby felt that she was inching closer to the identity of her secret admirer. It was as if she already knew who he was, yet somehow she couldn't quite name him.

"Any ideas?" Abby said after a few minutes.

"They remind me of something . . . or someone. . . ."

"Who? What?"

"You," Isabel concluded.

"*Me?*" Abby cried impatiently. "I know all about me. I want to know who *he* is!"

Isabel gave her another look. But she didn't say anything.

For that, Abby was grateful.

"These are all things that *you've* done," Isabel said slowly. "You've camped in a tent, you've baked and sold cookies, you've had diving contests with your friends. . . ."

"I haven't worn a tux," Abby interrupted. Then she stopped.

She knew who had.

A light tap on the door interrupted her thoughts. Eva came into the room. "What's everyone doing?"

"Looking at pictures," Isabel said.

Eva leaned over Isabel's shoulder to see.

"We're playing a guessing game," Isabel explained. "Do these pictures remind you of any of Abby's friends?"

"Jessica?" Eva said, referring to Abby's former best friend who had moved to the other side of the country.

"No, it has to be a boy," Isabel said.

Abby's face began to burn. "Never mind," she mumbled.

"And don't ask what it's about," Isabel went on, "because Abby won't tell you."

"Ah!" Eva's eyes lit up. "You have a boyfriend, Abby?"

"Of course not," Abby snapped. She was tired of being on the spot. "Do you?"

Eva didn't reply.

Isabel looked curiously at her twin. "*Do* you have a boyfriend, Eva?" she asked again.

For a moment, it seemed as if Eva wouldn't answer. But then she shrugged.

"So what if I do?" she said almost defiantly.

"I *knew* it!" Isabel cried.

"Me, too," Abby said. She wondered if any other members of the Hayes family had figured out Eva's secret.

"How long has this been going on?" Isabel asked.

"Just a few weeks," Eva admitted.

"'Just a few weeks?'" Isabel repeated. "And you didn't tell me? Your very own twin sister? Who is he?"

Eva whispered a name in her ear.

"*Him?*" Isabel looked shocked. She hadn't started dating yet. She was too busy with theater, debate club, school politics, and schoolwork to even think about boys.

At least that was what she always said.

"Tell me, too," Abby demanded.

Eva shook her head. "Not unless you explain what these pictures are all about."

"That's blackmail," Abby protested.

"Yes, so what?" Eva replied.

"Tell us!" Isabel urged.

Abby frowned at her two older sisters. "If I do, will you keep my secret?" she asked.

"Yes," they said in unison.

"You can trust us," Isabel said.

"Promise," Eva said.

"Okay, well . . ." Abby took a deep breath. "The truth is . . . I have a secret admirer. He's sent me almost a dozen valentines this week."

"Are you serious?" Isabel cried.

"Who is he?" Eva said.

"It's a secret admirer, *duh*," Isabel said to her. "That means Abby doesn't know."

"The pictures are clues," Abby explained. "At least I think they are. He's put them in the last few valentine cards. I feel like I *almost* know who he is."

"Casey or Mason," Eva said promptly. "It has to be one of the two."

"I agree," Isabel said. "These pictures show things you've done with your closest friends. And Casey and Mason are your only close friends who are also boys."

"You really think so?" Abby said. "Casey — well, I think he might like Hannah; and Mason . . ." Her voice trailed off.

A picture of Mason in a tux flashed in front of her eyes. He had worn it to usher in the fifth grade.

He had taken part in the diving contest, had tried to scare the girls when they slept in a tent in Abby's backyard, and was her cookie-selling partner.

And, of course, he knew all about T-Jeff.

Not to mention that he "knew" her secret admirer. . . .

"No, not Mason!" Abby cried.

"He's awfully cute," Eva said.

"And a good friend," Isabel added.

Abby buried her face in her hands. "I don't want it to be him!"

But somehow she knew that it was.

Chapter 10

> **Friday**
>
> "That's the secret to life . . . replace one worry with another. . . ."
>
> — Charles M. Schulz
>
> **Dishcloth Calendar**

Old worry: Who is my secret admirer?
New worry: OMG, it's Mason!!!

Old worry: What do I do about all the Smooch cards?
New worry: How do I tell Mason that I know it's him?
Another new worry: Should I be honest or pretend that I still don't know?

I need to think seriously about this.
<u>No!</u>

I've been thinking about it too much.
And besides, there are other worries in the
Hayes family.

After I told Eva and Isabel about my
secret admirer, and swore them to secrecy,
Eva told me the name of her boyfriend.

Old worry: What's wrong with Eva?
She's acting so strangely.
New worry: Eva and <u>Stephan</u>? Has she
lost her mind?

Eva is sporty, the captain of many teams,
and very popular.
Stephan is quiet, has one or two friends,
and only participates in "solo sports" like
hiking, skiing, or kayaking.
He has longish hair, is skinny, and has
friendly eyes.
He's totally opposite from Eva.
That's what Isabel said. She also said
that Stephan is a nice guy, but he just
isn't Eva's type!

And she should know. She's closer to Eva than anyone else.

She's worried that they don't have anything in common. She's worried that Eva's heart will be broken.

Or that Eva will break Stephan's heart.

Isabel seems sure that <u>someone</u> will soon be very unhappy.

I wonder if that's true.

I also wonder if that might be true of me and Mason. Will someone soon be very unhappy?

Old worry: How will I feel about my secret admirer?

New worry: How <u>do</u> I feel about Mason? Not as a friend, but as . . . something else.

When Abby arrived at school on Friday morning, Mason was waiting for her.

Of course, Abby thought.

When you didn't want to see someone, they were

always the first person you saw when you stepped out of the bus.

What was she supposed to do now?

What could she possibly say to him?

Hey, Mason! Put any Smooch cards in my locker today?

So, it's you.

Do you really like me?

No. She could never say any of those things. *Ever.*

"Abby!" Mason looked really happy to see her.

"Oh, hi," Abby said, pretending that she'd just noticed him. Her voice sounded strained and unnatural. "How are you, Mason?"

Oh, that was lame.

But he didn't seem to notice. He started chatting right away.

"Do you know that cows can climb up stairs but not down?" he asked.

"Cows can climb stairs . . . ?" Abby said. She was relieved that he wasn't talking about Smooch cards, but she couldn't exactly focus on cows. "That's so random."

"We could get a cow up to the second floor of the school, but then we wouldn't be able to get it back down," he explained.

"Is this a science project?"

"Just an interesting thought," he said.

"Mason, you're out of your mind," Abby said.

"I know," he said cheerfully.

Hannah joined them. Her eyes were sparkling. "Abby, have you gotten a Smooch card yet today?" she asked.

Abby felt the warmth rush to her face. "I haven't been to my locker yet," she mumbled.

Now she wished the conversation would return to cows and their habits.

But Hannah had only one thing on her mind. "Did you ask your sisters to help you discover who your secret admirer is?"

"You asked Isabel and Eva?" Mason said in astonishment.

"They *are* my sisters," Abby said. "And yes, I did."

She couldn't look Mason in the eye.

We looked at the clues together, she wanted to say, *and they told us everything we needed to know.*

But she couldn't. Not here, not now.

"They didn't help much," she fibbed. "They just teased me."

"Typical," Mason said.

"What about that boy from seventh period science?" Hannah said. "The one with the strange hair. Maybe he's your secret admirer."

"Tobias," Abby said. "No, it's *definitely* not him!"

"Are you sure?" Mason teased. "What if lots of guys are sending you Smooch cards?"

"Including you, Mason?" Abby couldn't help saying. She tried to keep a light tone, but her voice wobbled.

"I'm one of your biggest admirers."

Hannah laughed. "I bet you are, Mason!" she said.

Abby pushed open the front doors of the school.

"I'm sick of Valentine's Day, Smooch cards, and all the rest of it. Can we change the subject?" she said. "Please?"

"What shall we talk about?" Hannah asked.

"Cows?" Abby said.

"Are you serious?" Hannah said.

Mason made a mooing noise.

"He's cow crazy," Abby said.

When they reached Abby's locker, Mason lifted his hand to say good-bye.

"I'll see you at lunch?" he asked.

Abby couldn't help noticing how he looked at her. Why hadn't she seen it before?

"It's him," Abby whispered to Hannah as soon as Mason had disappeared around the corner.

Hannah twirled her locker combination. "Him?" she repeated.

"*Him,*" Abby said. "You know!"

"I have no idea what you're talking about, Abby."

Why was Hannah being so dense? Abby yanked open her locker. A Smooch card fell out.

"Another one!" Hannah cried. "Who is it?"

Abby looked at her friend and sighed.

Then, curious in spite of herself, she opened the envelope. The new Smooch card featured a bat surrounded by hearts.

"Weird," Hannah giggled. "But sort of funny, too."

I'M BATTY ABOUT YOU, the message read. There was also another clue: a photo of autumn leaves.

"Of course," Abby said under her breath. She and Mason had raked leaves together last year. "It's definitely him."

"*Him?*" Hannah repeated. "You mean your secret admirer?"

"I've been *trying* to tell you!" Abby said.

How could she not see? It was so obvious to Abby now.

"It's Mason," Abby said. "He's my secret admirer."

Later:

When I told her that Mason was my secret admirer, Hannah didn't believe it at first.

I had to spend about ten minutes convincing her that it was true.

"But it can't be Mason!" she said over and over. "He's been helping us figure it out. . . ."

"Yeah," I said. "I know."

"And besides, he doesn't act like he has a crush on you. . . . Are you sure it's him?"

"All the clues add up," I told her. "The cookies, the tux, the diving board, the leaves . . ."

Hannah shook her head. "This isn't the Mason I know."

"Me, neither," I agreed. "He's way too sneaky."

"Sneaky? I'm talking adorable and romantic," Hannah said. "Who knew?"

When I told Sophia, she was surprised, too. But she believed me right away.

"Wow, Mason fooled us all," she said. "He's a good actor. And so sweet! I didn't realize . . ." Her voice trailed off.

"Realize what?"

"Nothing," Sophia said.

"Do you have a crush on Mason?"

"No way!" Sophia blushed. "But he is awfully cute!"

Was he cute? I've never thought of the Big Burper that way.

Adorable? Maybe, but in the way that your best friend is adorable.

Romantic? Who, Mason?

He lied to me. And I didn't think he could do that. He's mostly very honest.

He even laughed and teased me about my secret admirer. He pretended to help us figure out who it was.

So who is this Mason, anyway?

I'm starting to feel as if I don't know him at all.

And I don't know how I feel about him anymore.

He feels like a stranger to me.

I feel like a stranger to myself!

Chapter 11

Friday

"A goal without a plan is
just a wish."

— Antoine de Saint-Exupéry

Wings Calendar

<u>My goal</u>:
To let Mason know that I <u>know</u>.

Why?
I just have to.
I can't go on pretending.

<u>My plan to tell Mason</u>:

Um . . .
I guess I don't have one.
This is more of a wish than a plan.
I need a solid plan!

My friends are trying to help me.

Hannah's plan:

She offered to tell Mason herself.
"You mean . . . ?" I said.
"Yes," Hannah said. "I will tell Mason
that you know he's your secret admirer."
"Oh, thank you!" I cried.
I imagined Hannah having a confidential
heart-to-heart chat with Mason in a private
corner somewhere.
I hugged her. "You're the best friend ever."
"It's nothing," Hannah said. "But let's
rehearse it first. So I get it right."
"I'll play Mason!" Sophia said.
"I'll watch," I said. I settled myself in
a chair.
Hannah pretended to see "Mason" in the
hallway. She marched right up to him.
"Good," I said.
Then she shook a finger in his face.
"The game's up," she said. "We're onto
you." She looked at me. "How's that?"

"Um, not quite right," I said. "Try again. Make it friendlier."

Hannah took a deep breath.

Then she smiled at "Mason." "We know who you are," she said. "We've figured out the clues."

Sophia looked like she was trying to keep a straight face. "You have?"

"We know that you're Abby's secret admirer."

"Show me your badge and I'll come quietly," Sophia joked.

Hannah's shoulders slumped. "It's not very good, is it?"

Then all three of us started to laugh.

Sophia's plan:

Did not involve talking to Mason.

Involved buying cards and slipping them into Mason's locker.

"It's very easy," Sophia explained. "You won't have to say a word to him. And neither will I or anyone else."

That sounded good.

"But how will Mason find out that I know . . . ?"

"You'll sign the cards," Sophia said. "You write something like 'Love from your crush, Abby.'"

"Are you out of your mind?" I cried. "I'm not writing anything like that!"

"Then just sign them, 'Your crush, Abby.'"

"No way!" I said. "I don't even want to send Mason a Smooch card. I'm not exactly in love with him, you know!"

"I was just trying to help," Sophia said.

"Well, thanks," I said. "It's a good plan, but not for me."

Then I came up with my own plan.

Abby's plan:

I am going to follow Mason around.

I will catch him in the act of slipping a Smooch card in my locker and then I'll yell out, "Aha!"

Or, maybe I'll say, "Eureka!"

Or just, "You, Mason?"

I'll pretend to be so surprised!

Mason will be relieved that I've figured it out. He'll grin and shrug and say, "What took you so long?"

Both Hannah and Sophia agreed this was a good plan.

For the rest of the day, I will secretly keep an eye on Mason.

It might be hard to do. Mason always seems to notice me. I'm never invisible when he's around.

Yet more proof that he's my secret admirer!

On the Mason Trail:

12:13 p.m. As usual, we all had lunch together.

I noticed that Mason laughed at all my jokes — even when they weren't funny.

(He must really like me.)

12:37 p.m. When he thought I wasn't looking, Mason bought three new Smooch cards. He hid them in his backpack.

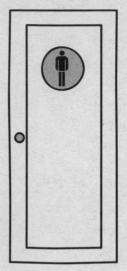

12:39 p.m. I followed Mason to the door of the . . . bathroom?

Oops.

12:48 p.m. Exciting moment! I saw Mason heading toward my locker. Finally I was going to catch him in the act!

12:49 p.m. Just as I was tiptoeing up behind him, Brianna grabbed my arm. She had "very important" news to share.

Guess what? Brianna has received so many valentine cards and presents that her family is going to rent a storage locker!

12:52 p.m. Wrenched self away from Brianna.

12:53 p.m. At my locker. Mason nowhere in sight.

12:54 p.m. Found a new Smooch card.

It's him. If I had any doubt before, I'm one hundred percent sure now.

1:42 p.m. Followed Mason to his science class. Was late for my next class.

2:23 p.m. Saw Mason duck into the nurse's office.

Is he sick? Does he have a hangnail, a headache, or a sprained wrist? Or is he suffering from love?

2:56 p.m. It's finally the end of the school day. Hurried through crowded hallway after Mason.

2:57 p.m. He arrived at my locker.

2:57-1/2 p.m. He took an envelope from one of his books and was about to slip it inside my locker door when I reached out and grabbed his arm.

The envelope fell to the floor.

Mason whirled around.

For a moment, we stared at each other.

Then Mason turned and ran.

I picked up the envelope he had dropped and opened it.

It was another Smooch card. Of course.

Chapter 12

Something unexpected has happened. Since I discovered him in the act of slipping a Smooch card into my locker, Mason has avoided me.

If I'm nearby, Mason won't look backward, forward, upward, down, around, left, right, or center!

The only direction he'll look is away from me!

Today, for the first time in ages, he didn't join me, Hannah, and Sophia for lunch.

The four of us had been having so much fun together lately. We joked around in gym and art class, sat together every day at lunch, walked each other to class...

I felt terrible.

I tried to explain what happened to my friends.

"I thought he'd laugh," I said. "Or that he'd make a joke out of it. I never thought that he'd be so upset."

"It's love," Sophia explained.

"Love? He won't meet my eyes. He won't talk to me or say hello," I went on. "If he sees me in the hallway, he looks away. When we have classes together, he sits on the other side of the room."

"It's upsetting," Sophia said. "But he'll get over it."

She seemed very certain.

"Will he?" I said. "I really, really hope so."

I almost felt like crying. Was this what love did to people? Ruin their friendships?

"Did I do the wrong thing?" I asked my friends. "Should I have pretended to know nothing?"

"No," Hannah said. "It would have come out sooner or later."

That should have made me feel better, but it didn't.

Even if I don't think I like Mason "that way," I still really like him! He's a close friend and I care about him.

I didn't want to embarrass him. I didn't want to hurt his feelings!

I really don't want to lose his friendship.

Who else do I joke with as much? Who else hangs around with me all the time?

Almost all my memories include Mason. We go back to kindergarten together!

"You're awfully quiet tonight, Abby," her father said as the family finished their dinner. "Is everything okay?"

Abby shrugged. Everything *wasn't* okay.

But she couldn't talk about it to the whole family all at once.

Maybe she'd say something to Isabel or Eva later. Maybe she'd ask their advice again. Maybe they'd be able to help her.

Isabel gave her a friendly nudge under the table. "How's you-know-who?" she whispered.

"*What?*" Alex said. His hearing was way too sharp for a third grader. "Who?"

"It's girl talk, Alex," Isabel said.

Abby blushed. "Can we change the subject?"

Fortunately, there were other family problems tonight.

"You didn't eat much dinner tonight, Eva," their mother observed. "Are you feeling all right?"

"Of course, Mom!" Eva said. "I'm fine. Never felt better." She stood up and began to clear the dishes.

"I saw your light on late last night," their father said. "Are you having trouble sleeping?"

Eva set the dishes down with a clatter. "I'm perfectly well!" she said. "There's absolutely nothing to worry about."

"Not eating, not sleeping?" their mother said with a frown. "That's not 'nothing.'"

Eva opened her mouth to reply. But before she could say anything, the doorbell rang.

"It's for me!" she cried, rushing out of the room.

"She's really okay," Isabel said to her parents. "Trust me."

"Are you sure?" her mother asked.

"*Yes,*" Isabel said.

Eva came back into the dining room. She looked transformed. Her face was glowing.

"Mom, Dad, I want you to meet someone," Eva said. She held her hand out. "This is Stephan."

Isabel nudged Abby under the table.

"It's *him,*" Abby whispered.

"I can't believe she's bringing him here," Isabel said under her breath. "She must be in love."

"Well, yeah," Abby whispered back.

Her father stood up and shook Stephan's hand. "How do you do, young man?" he said.

Young man? Abby had never heard her father call anyone "young man" before.

"Mr. Hayes," Stephan said, smiling. "Mrs. Hayes. Nice to meet you."

Well, he was polite, anyway.

Parents always liked that.

Abby tried to imagine what would happen if she invited Mason over one evening.

Would her father shake Mason's hand?

Would Mason say, "Nice to meet you, Mr. and Mrs. Hayes?"

Of course not. He had been at their house constantly for years.

Her parents wouldn't even notice him. Or if they
did, they'd joke with him. They'd say, "Hey, it's you.
Don't eat all our cookies."

"Welcome to our home," Abby's mother was saying to Stephan. "It's very good to meet you."

Alex stared as if Stephan were an alien who had
just gotten off a spaceship.

"I still don't get it," Isabel muttered, darting glances
at her sister and Stephan. "How can she be in love
with him? He's so different from her."

"That's love," Abby said, repeating what Sophia
had told her. "It doesn't always make sense."

It didn't make sense that Mason had such a crush
on her, either. It didn't make sense that Abby didn't
have a crush on *him*.

Nothing about love seemed to make sense.

Isabel snorted.

"He looks really nice," Abby whispered. Stephan
had a friendly, quiet manner and an open smile. "And
we know he's brave since he's meeting all of us at
once," she added.

Isabel rolled her eyes. "We're not *that* scary."

"Oh, yeah?" Abby muttered. Even *she* got scared by her family, sometimes.

Eva stepped forward and took Stephan's hand. "Stephan and I are going to a movie together," she announced.

"It's a school night," her mother pointed out.

Normally, Eva would have snapped, "I *know*!"

But tonight, she said sweetly instead, "My homework is all done, Mom and Dad. Stephan's dad will drive us there and back. I'll be home by ten thirty."

For once, the Hayes parents were speechless.

As Eva and Stephan turned to go, her mother called out, "Have a good time!"

The front door slammed shut. Their father let out a long breath.

"Are you next, Isabel?" he asked. "Do you have any surprises in store for us?"

"No!" Isabel said. "I've got too much schoolwork."

"Then Abby's next," Alex said.

"Abby is *way* too young to start thinking about boys," her mother said. "Aren't you, Abby?"

Abby and Isabel exchanged a quick look.

"I guess," Abby mumbled. "But there are lots of girls in my class who are interested."

And it wasn't just Brianna and Victoria, either. There was Sophia. And Hannah might be interested — a little, at least — in Casey.

Were they too young? Abby wondered. *Am I too young?*

She couldn't imagine acting the way Eva did.

She wouldn't take Mason's hand in front of her entire family.

She wouldn't introduce him as her date.

She wouldn't be so radiant when he walked in the room.

She wouldn't lose sleep or her appetite. She wouldn't spend hours on the phone.

But Eva was in love. Abby wasn't.

That had nothing to do with being too young. It was because she didn't have a crush on Mason.

It was clear to her now. Especially after seeing Eva and Stephan.

Would she feel differently one day?

Abby couldn't be sure, but she didn't think so.

Chapter 13

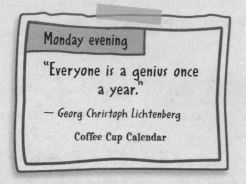

Is today my genius day? I hope so. I need to come up with an A+ brilliant plan.

My brilliant plan must do many things:

1. It must let Mason know that I'm his friend.

2. It must also let him know that I <u>don't</u> have a crush on him.

3. Here's the hard part — I don't want to hurt his feelings!

4. Can I tell the truth without wrecking our friendship forever?

5. Help! I want our old, easy, comfortable friendship back!

This is not going to be easy.

What if today isn't my genius day?
What if I don't come up with a plan?
What if Mason continues to avoid me?
What if our friendship is over forever?

Idea #1
Tear out this page and give it to Mason.
  But I'd have to scribble out that part about "not hurting his feelings." I might have to cross out some other stuff, too.
  Never mind!

I'm staring into space again. No more ideas.
  What if that one is the only one I'm going to get?

So frustrated I just tossed my journal on the bed and paced around the room.
  Aha! I have another idea!

* * *

Idea #2
Send him a text message.
But can I explain myself in a few words?
Um, I don't think so. . . .

Idea #3
Post something on his family Web page?
WAY too public!

Idea #4
Uh . . .

I guess today is NOT my genius day.
But I really wish that it was.
I give up on trying to find ideas.
Instead, I am flipping through my journal
and reading quotes from the last few
weeks.
"Every picture tells a story." This quote
makes me think.
The Smooch cards told a story, and so
did the pictures that Mason put inside
the cards.

AHA! *No, it's not an idea. It's a* thought.

There is something very strange going on.

Did Mason want me to know that he was my secret admirer?

Or didn't he?

I mean, he sent me so many clues.

He <u>must</u> have wanted me to find out. He must have expected me to put together the puzzle sooner or later.

So why did he get so upset when I finally did?

This makes no sense at all!

Unless . . . he was hoping to tell me himself?

Or perhaps he thought I'd let him know in a different way?

Like, by sending him my own Smooch card? Or by asking him out or by telling him I liked him, too. . . .

But I could never do that —
Wait a minute. . . .
EUREKA!
A genius idea! <u>Gotcha</u>!

Idea #5*

Find supercute photo of Mason and me as little kids.

The photo shows us as kindergartners having a water fight in a plastic pool.

Place supercute photo inside adorable purple polka-dotted blank greeting card.

Write message to Mason. Try to put all my feelings inside it. Cross fingers, seal with lots of hope.

Stick a star sticker on the envelope.

Slip into Mason's locker first thing Tuesday morning.

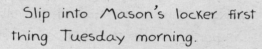

*Hey, this idea deserves a better name than #5.

Shall I call it First Good Idea? The Front-Runner? The Winner?

Oh, who cares what it's called! I just hope it works!

"It is possible to fail in many ways . . . while to succeed is possible in only one way."

— Aristotle

Mashed Potato Calendar

Did I find the one way to succeed?
Or have I failed in many ways?

<u>Ways to Fail (Let Me Count Them)</u>:

1. Was my message written badly?
2. Did I pick the wrong words?
3. Was my signature too large or too small?
4. Should I have picked another picture of Mason and me?
5. Should I have used a heart instead of a star sticker?
6. Should I have . . . oh, never mind!

*   *   *

Tuesday, mid-morning:

Saw Mason in the hallway. Did he wave to me? Or was he waving to someone just behind me?

Tuesday, late morning

Passed Mason in hallway again. He seemed to be smiling in my direction. I waved wildly at him just in case.

Tuesday, lunch

Hannah, Sophia, and I are slowly eating our sandwiches when Mason sits down next to me.

I squeeze hard on my sandwich. Jelly squirts onto the table and over my sweatshirt.

Nice. Now I have jelly all over the table and my clothes.

And Mason is sitting next to me.

Sophia and Hannah keep looking at each other.

Are they wondering whether to wipe off the table?

Or do they want to tell me I have jelly on my face?

No, they're plotting an escape.

They suddenly rise from their seats and flee to the other side of the cafeteria.

I'm alone with Mason.

Tuesday, lunch - Part 2:

Awkward conversation #1:
Me: Um, hi!
Mason: Hi!
Me: Hey!

Silence.

Awkward Conversation #2:
Me: Did you . . . uh . . .
Mason: Yeah, uh . . .
Me: Is?

*   *   *

Silence.

Awkward Conversation #3:
Mason: Cool!
Me: What?
Mason: You know . . .
Me: No.

Silence.

Awkward Conversation #4:
Mason: Would you like to go to the dance with me?
Me: The dance? But –

Silence.

Awkward Conversation #5:
Me: Did you get my card?
Mason: Yes.
Me: I can't, Mason. You know why.
Mason: No, you don't understand.
Me: Me? I do, it's you who doesn't . . .

*   *   *

Silence.

Awkward Conversation #6:
Mason: I want you to come to the dance as my friend.
Me: Do you really mean that?
Mason: You're one of my best friends. You always will be.
Me: Really?
Mason: Yes.
Me: Well, you are, too. But —
Mason: I know. It's okay.
Me: Really?
Mason: Yes. Someday . . .
Me: Do I still have jelly on my face?
Mason: Yes.

And then the bell rings. I wipe the jelly from my face. We walk to class together.

Tuesday, after lunch

I am relieved.
I am so relieved.

Mason and I are friends again.
<u>Hooray!</u>

Tuesday, afternoon

- I am SO relieved!
Should I go to the dance with him? As just friends?

Tuesday, late afternoon

I think that maybe I will.

Chapter 14

The Valentine's Day dance was held in the cafeteria. Teachers and parents stood against the walls, watching us. But the room was dim, so we hardly noticed them. All the chairs and tables were gone. The room was lit by flashing colored lights.

When Mason and I came in, the dance floor was already packed. We danced into the center of the crowd.

I saw all my friends. Sophia was dancing with a lot of different boys. Hannah was dancing with three other girls.

There was a live band performing on a wooden stage at the end of the cafeteria.

They were called Boy Blizzard, and Simon was playing the saxophone!

Brianna was flirting with Simon and trying to convince him to let her sing a song. But he kept shaking his head.

After a minute, I forgot all about Simon.

There were so many friends to greet. There were so many people to dance with!

After the first few minutes, Mason and I got separated. When I saw him next, he was dancing with Sophia. I was dancing with Lucas.

It was surprisingly enjoyable. And he didn't mention depressing poems once!

The dance itself was a lot more relaxed and fun than I expected. Almost no one was paired up. Nobody acted too romantic or possessive.

I wonder if high school dances are this much fun? Or do you have to be a couple to enjoy them?

Oh, who cares? The important thing is . . . I had a great time!

After I danced with Lucas, Mason danced with Hannah, and I danced with Casey.

Then all of us danced together . . . separately . . . together again.

The room was a blur of noise, friends, flashing lights, and loud music.

And then, before I realized it, the dance was over. . . .

My father drove us home.

Before he got out of the car, Mason slipped one last Smooch card into my hand.

"Uh-oh," I said.

"Don't worry," he said. "It's not like that."

We didn't say any more. I put the envelope in my coat pocket and waited until I was alone in my room to open it.

Inside the envelope was a card with a photograph of some trees.

Mason had written, "Thanks for coming to the dance with me. I'm glad we're friends."

So am I.

Now I'm sitting in my writing loft. I'm too wide-awake to sleep. I keep hearing Boy Blizzard's music in my head. I keep seeing the laughing faces of my classmates. I keep remembering whirling around the dance floor with all my friends.

But happily, I'm not dreaming about Simon. Or worrying about Mason.

Maybe in a few years, I'll be happy to have a date. But I don't need to worry about that yet.

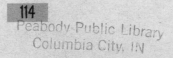

FIND OUT HOW IT ALL BEGAN!

HERE'S A PEEK AT
THE AMAZING DAYS OF
ABBY HAYES #1:
EVERY CLOUD HAS A
SILVER LINING

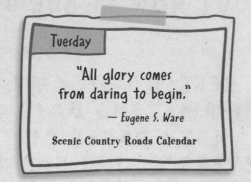

Or being forced to begin.

I wish we could just skip fifth grade and go straight to middle school.

Abby looked at her list of school supplies.

List of school supplies needed for Ms. Kantor's fifth-grade class:

Pencils boring!

Pens, blue and red Why not green and red? Or purple and orange? Brought my favorite purple pen to school anyway. Purple rebellion!

Crayons NO! No! I am tired of coloring.

I have been coloring since age two. No
more coloring with crayons – P-L-E-A-S-E!!!!

**Paper, two-pocket folders, ruler, pencil
sharpener** ho hum, supplies as usual

A box of tissues Will we be crying?

List of supplies I wish
we needed:
Rainbow pens
Souvenirs from vacation
(seashells, calendars,
rocks . . .)

Lined paper in fluorescent
colors
Favorite books
CDs and personal stereos
Earrings for all girls

"Let's go around the class and introduce ourselves,"
said Ms. Kantor. "Let's start with me. I'm Ms. Kantor,
your fifth-grade teacher. Last year I taught at Swiss
Hill Elementary. I have two children. My hobbies are
astronomy, canoeing, and speaking French."

Abby sat in the row across from Jessica. Her notebook was on her lap.

Ms. Kantor's hair is dark blond. Her nose is pointy. I can't tell if she's going to be nice or not, but so far she's okay.

"My voice may give out later today," Ms. Kantor said. "This happens every year during the first week of school. I have to get used to talking in class!" She cleared her throat.

Ms. Kantor cleared her throat again. Abby hoped that she wouldn't do this all year long. One week was going to be bad enough.

"Who's next? Say your name and tell us something about yourself."

Brianna stood up. Her toenails were painted glittery orange. She was wearing bell-bottoms and a velour T-shirt. "I'm Brianna," she announced, tossing her hair like an actress on a soap opera. "I love horseback riding, soccer, and dancing."

Brianna Brag Ratio: One brag to two sentences. (Usual Brianna Brag Ratio: Twenty brags to one sentence.)

"Yay, Brianna," Bethany said, then stood up. "I'm Bethany, Brianna's best friend." She sat down again.

"Can you tell us a little more about yourself, Bethany?" Ms. Kantor asked.

"I like to ice-skate, and I have a hamster," Bethany said, pulling at her earrings. They were tiny silver skates that dangled from her ears like charms.

Bethany is Brianna's personal cheerleader. She dresses like Brianna, looks like Brianna (except hair is blond, not dark), and acts like Brianna. Who says that science has not yet cloned a human being? They haven't met Brianna and Bethany!

Zach and Tyler stood up at the same time. "We like electronic games and computers," they chanted in unison.

"They're cute," Brianna whispered loudly to Bethany.

"No Game Boys in school," Ms. Kantor warned, pointing to Zach's backpack.

No Game Boys in school???!!! Z and T are going to be miserable. Last year they brought their games every day to play at recess and after school. If they have to leave them at home, they will wither and sicken.

P.S. Did I hear Brianna say that Z and T are cute? Ugh!!! What is so cute about them? They are loud, dumb, and obsessed with technology!

The other students introduced themselves in turn. Meghan and Rachel had gone away to sleep-away camp. Jon had played basketball and visited Norway with his family.

There was a new girl in the class. Her family had moved to town just a few weeks ago. Her name was Natalie. She was small and thin, with short dark hair. "I like to read," she said in a quiet voice. "My favorite books are the Harry Potter books. I've read them each nine times. I also have a chemistry set. I like to do experiments."

As she sat down, she caught Abby's eye and smiled quickly, then looked away.

New girl seems nice. Not loud and bragging like Brianna and Bethany. Maybe she wants to eat lunch with Jessica and me. Wonder if she has a good dessert to trade? Note to self: Must stop thinking about desserts! This is not the way to become a soccer star!

It was Jessica's turn. For the first day of school she had worn overalls and a black tank top. She had pinned peace signs and little hearts all over the overall straps. Her hair was in a ponytail.

She pulled out a photo of a spaceship. "This is what I want to do when I get older," she said. "I plan to be an astronaut. I also have asthma, love apricot jam, and Abby is my best friend."

"Very nice, Jessica," Ms. Kantor said. "Next?"

Abby jumped to her feet. "I'm Abby!" Suddenly she couldn't think of a thing to say. That she had a calendar collection? Too weird. That she wanted to be a star soccer player? Not yet. That she had three SuperSibs? The less said about them the better. Who was she, anyway?

"Um, my best friend is um, Jessica. . . . Um, this year my parents are, um, letting me, um, bike to the store by myself. . . . I love to write!" she finished in a burst of inspiration.

Spend the day with Abby!

Read them all!